PLEASE WASH
YOUR HANDS
BEFORE YOU READ ME
AND KEEP ME CLEAN

D1366796

My Mom Made Me Go to Camp

My Mom Made Me Go to Camp

by Judy Delton
pictures by Lisa McCue

Delacorte
Press

Published by
Delacorte Press
Bantam Doubleday Dell Publishing Group, Inc.
666 Fifth Avenue
New York, New York 10103

Book design by Robin Arzt

Library of Congress Cataloging in Publication Data
Delton, Judy.
My mom made me go to camp / by Judy Delton ; illustrated by Lisa McCue.
p. cm.
Summary: Archie's negative feelings about camp change after he catches a fish and learns how to swim.
ISBN 0-385-30040-9
ISBN 0-385-30113-8 (lib. ed.)
[1. Camps—Fiction.] I. McCue, Lisa, ill. II. Title.
PZ7.D388Mym 1990
[E]—dc20 89-23358 CIP AC
Printed in Italy
June 1990
10 9 8 7 6 5 4 3 2 1
NIL

For Lori Mack, again
With love,
J.D.

To my mom
With love,
L.M.

"Summer is coming," said my mother one morning.
"The grass is getting green and the robins are back in town."

"School will be out, and I can play all day," I said.

"And this year you can go to camp," said my mom.
"At Horseshoe Lake."

GREAT TASTE
JELLY

“Camp?” I said. “I’m not old enough to go to camp.”

“Sure you are,” said my mom. “Camp is fun. You will weave baskets and swim and fish and learn the names of wildflowers. You will put up a tent and gather firewood. You will roast hot dogs and marshmallows over an open fire.”

The marshmallows sounded like fun.

The grass got greener. The sun got warmer.
Flowers started coming up in our yard.
And school was out.
I knew it was summer.

"We have to shop for your camp things," said my mother.

"What things?" I said.

"Shoes and a swimsuit and a sleeping bag. Shorts and bug spray and a first-aid kit."

"I don't want to sleep in a sleeping bag. I hate bugs. And I don't want any first aid."

"You'll have a good time," said my mother. "We have a lot to do. I have to sew labels in all of your clothes."

ARCHIE

"Don't they know who I am?" I cried.
"I don't want to be labeled!"

"That's just in case you lose your things,"
she said.

"Or if they lose ME," I muttered.

Soon it was time to go to camp.
It was pouring rain.
I didn't know anybody.
And my new sneakers gave me a blister.

“Good-bye!” called my mother, outside of the bus window.

“Have a good time! Don’t go into deep water! Be careful near the fire! Take your vitamin pill! Write me a postcard!”

The bus started and soon my mother was just a little dot in front of the drugstore. I was on my way to camp.

CAM

When we got to camp, we had beans for supper.

I hate beans.

Then we sang around the campfire.

I hate to sing.

And when we went to bed, mosquitoes
buzzed around my cot.
Just mine.
I hate mosquitoes.
Three bit me. Even with the bug spray.

In the morning we had swimming lessons.

"Yeah!" said a girl named Jill. "I love to swim."

The lifeguard showed us how to swim.

He held each of us in the water.

When he let go of Jill, she swam.

And David swam.

Even a little bitty kid named Shorty swam.

But when the lifeguard let go of me, I sank like a rock.

Right to the bottom of Horseshoe Lake.

"Boy!" I said. "I thought horseshoes brought luck."

I wrote a postcard to my mom. It said, "I want to come home."

After lunch we went for a hike in the woods.
Brian found a four-leaf clover.
Shorty found a bird's nest.
Jill said, "Look. A real Indian arrowhead!"
All I got was a rash.
It was red.
It itched.

I wrote my mom another postcard.
"I've got a disease," it said. "Come and get me right away."

That night a bat got in our tent.
Jill screamed, "I'm scared of them!" She hid under the cot.
Shorty chased it, but he couldn't catch it.
I grabbed the fishnet and trapped the bat inside.
Then I took it outside and let it go.

The kids all clapped.
Jill yelled, "Archie saved us!"
(That's my name, Archie.)

DEAR

I wrote a postcard to my mom.
"We had beans again," it said. "I hate beans. I'm still itching. And I can't swim. But tonight I caught a bat. Wait until tomorrow to come and get me."

The next day we went fishing.
Jill caught a minnow.
Brian caught an old boot.
But I caught a sunfish.
He was big enough to save.
The cook fried him for me for supper.
(At least I didn't have to eat beans again.)

That night Jill cried all night.
She was homesick.
Shorty cried too.
Lots of kids wanted their mothers.
It was awful.
The only kid who wasn't homesick was me.

"Dear Mom," I wrote on a postcard.
"The bugs are still bad. But I'm learning to swim. I caught a big fish. And I'm the only one who isn't homesick around here."

It was the last day of camp and I could swim three feet without sinking.
The bug spray was beginning to work.
Brian said he would write to me when camp was over.

The bus ride home was fast and bumpy. When I got off the bus my mom was there to meet me.

"You are sunburned!" she said.
"Did you miss me? Were the children nice? Did you stay out of deep water? Did you have a good time at camp?"

"It was okay," I said.
"But we didn't roast marshmallows. Not even once."

Judy Delton has written more than sixty-five books for young readers, including the Dell Young Yearling books about the Pee Wee Scouts. She lives in St. Paul, Minnesota.

Lisa McCue has illustrated several books for children, including *Hired Help for Rabbit*, by Judy Delton (Macmillan). She lives in Bethlehem, Pennsylvania.